The Night Before Christmas

By Clement C. Moore

Illustrated by Larry Eldredge

The Night Before Christmas

 was the night

 before Christmas,

when all through the house

Not a creature was stirring,

not even a mouse.

The stockings were hung

by the chimney with care,

In hopes that St. Nicholas

soon would be there.

The children were nestled all snug in their beds,
While visions of sugarplums danced in their heads;

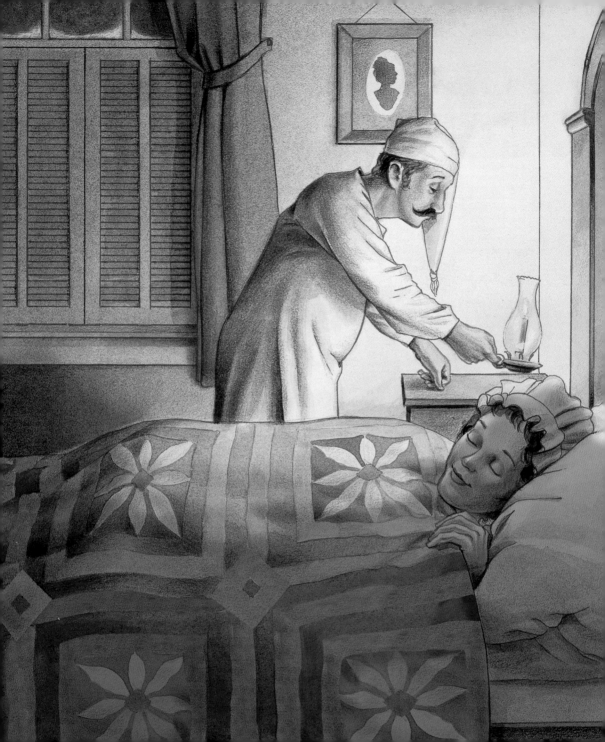

And mamma in her

kerchief and I in my cap

Had just settled down

for a long winter's nap—

When out on the lawn

there arose such a clatter

I sprang from my bed

to see what was the matter.

way to the window

I flew like a flash,

Tore open the shutter

and threw up the sash.

The moon on the breast

of the new-fallen snow

Gave a luster of midday

to objects below;

hen what
to my wondering
eyes should appear
But a miniature sleigh
and eight tiny reindeer,
With a little old driver
so lively and quick,
I knew in a moment
it must be St. Nick!

ore rapid than eagles

his coursers they came,

And he whistled and shouted

and called them by name.

"Now, Dasher! Now, Dancer!

Now, Prancer and Vixen!

On, Comet! On, Cupid!

On, Donder and Blitzen!—

o the top of the porch,

to the top of the wall,

Now dash away, dash away,

dash away all!"

As dry leaves that before

the wild hurricane fly,

When they meet with an

obstacle mount to the sky,

So up to the housetop

the coursers they flew,

With a sleigh full of toys—

and St. Nicholas too.

nd then in a twinkling

I heard on the roof

The prancing and pawing

of each little hoof.

As I drew in my head

and was turning around,

Down the chimney

St. Nicholas came with a bound.

He was dressed all in fur

from his head to his foot,

And his clothes were all tarnished

with ashes and soot.

A bundle of toys he had

flung on his back,

And he looked like a peddler

just opening his pack.

is eyes, how they twinkled!

His dimples, how merry!

His cheeks were like roses,

his nose like a cherry;

His droll little mouth

was drawn up like a bow,

And the beard on his chin

was as white as the snow.

The stump of a pipe

he held tight in his teeth,

And the smoke, it encircled

his head like a wreath.

He had a broad face

and a little round belly

That shook when he laughed,

like a bowl full of jelly.

He was chubby and plump—

a right jolly old elf,

And I laughed when I saw him,

in spite of myself;

 wink of his eye

and a twist of his head

Soon gave me to know

I had nothing to dread.

He spoke not a word

but went straight to his work

And filled all the stockings,

then turned with a jerk,

 nd laying his finger

aside of his nose

And giving a nod,

up the chimney he rose.

He sprang to his sleigh,

to his team gave a whistle,

And away they all flew

like the down of a thistle.

 ut I heard him exclaim,

ere they drove out of sight,

"Happy Christmas to all

and to all a good night!"